Dinosaur eggs

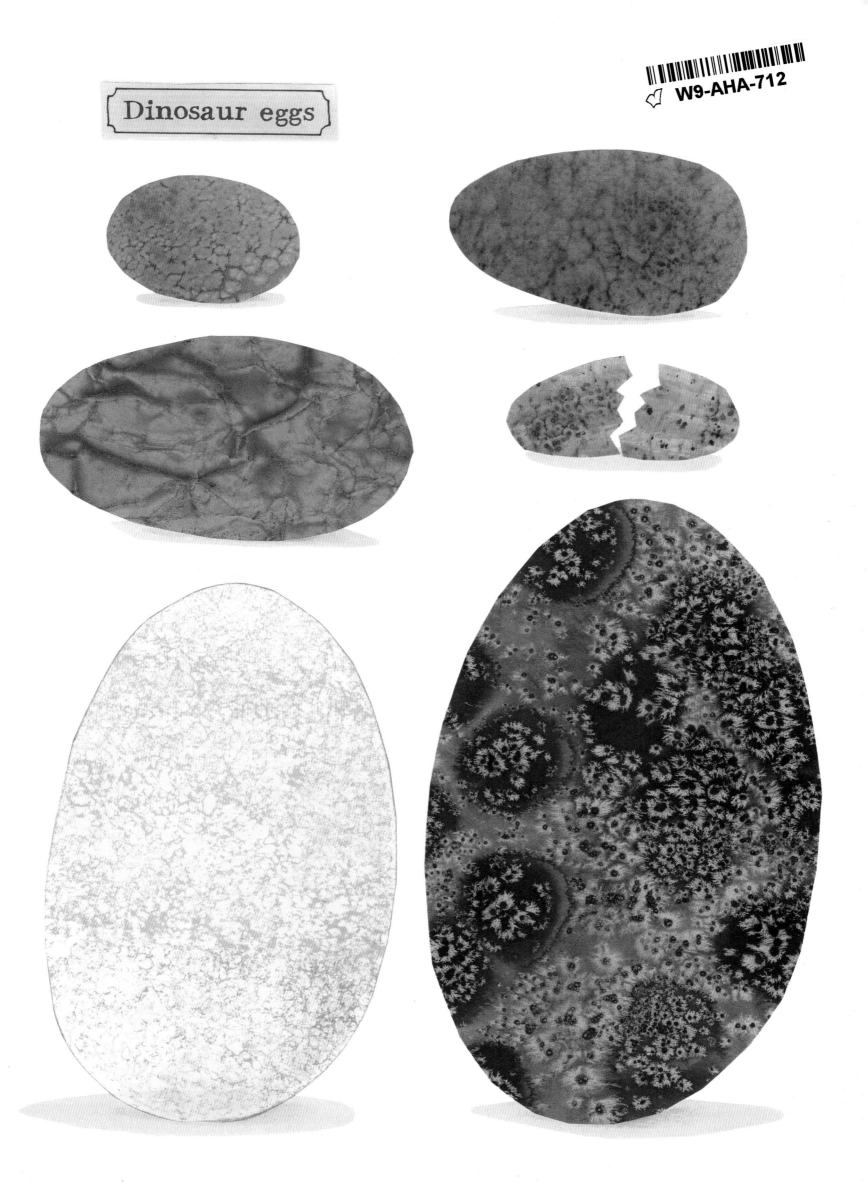

Originally published as *Het ongelooflijke maar waargebeurde verhaal over de dino's* in Belgium and Holland
by Clavis Uitgeverij, Hasselt—Amsterdam, 2018
English translation from the Dutch by Clavis Publishing Inc., New York

Visit us on the Web at www.clavisbooks.com.

The Truth About Dinosaurs written and illustrated by Guido Van Genechten

ISBN 978-1-60537-423-9

This book was printed in March 2018 at DENONA d.o.o., Zagreb, Marina Getaldica 1, Croatia.

First Edition
10 9 8 7 6 5 4 3 2 1

THE TRUTH ABOUT DINOSAURS

Guido Van Genechten

Clavis
NEW YORK

cluck
cluck

EXCUSE ME, MA'AM, BUT I THINK YOU'RE
IN THE WRONG STORY.

Me? No, why? This is my story!

BUT THIS IS A STORY ABOUT DINOSAURS,
AND YOU'RE A CHICKEN.

A what? You've really offended me, you know.
Obviously I'm a dinosaur! Look at my feet. These are dinosaur feet, right?
Chicken? Hmmph . . . You mean GALLUS GALLUS DOMESTICUS!

You don't believe me? Wait, I'll get some proof.

The Velociraptor Family

Mommy Loci and Daddy Rapt take a ride together

Little Velo loves his new scooter

There! My photo album, a family heirloom. I got it from my grandma
(and she got it from *her* grandma). Look—here you see the Velociraptors.
They are my great-great-great-great-great-great-great-great-great-great-
great-great-grand-family. Do you recognize the feet?

75,000,000 B.C.

TICKET
28.6
POUNDS

Grandpa takes a stroll

And they had feathers too. But they couldn't fly.
Just flap their wings a little, like we still do.
They were super-fast runners and very smart.

The Iguanodon Family

CASA CARA
32

TICKET 10,072 POUNDS

Home Sweet Home

HOORAY FOUR BABIES

These are the Iguanodons. They are distant relatives of my daddy.
The adults weighed up to 10,000 pounds. That's as much as three heavy cars!

A refreshing dip

The family gets bigger and bigger

As you can see, they also lay eggs.
But, um . . . Iguanodon eggs were a bit bigger than mine.

The Diplodocus Family

Our first Diplodo-kiss

Moving day

Another side of the family, the Diplodocuses.
They were very big, very tall, and very strong . . .
but they were also very sweet.

JURA

Our honeymoon

What a view!

TICKET 26,616 POUNDS

A flower
for Dip

MARRIAGE LICENSE

FOR EVER

Docus and Dip
are from this day forward together

At last

Look up there—two Diplodocuses are kissing under a full moon!
They decided to spend their lives together. So sweet!
Then they went on a fabulous honeymoon.

The Tyrannosaurus Family

Rex

TICKET 17,903 POUNDS

Oh dear—my cousin Tyrannosaurus!

They were more into roaring than kissing.

Take a close look at the gigantic jaws of Rex. He had very sharp teeth.

Each tooth was as big as a banana!

But of course, even Tyrannosaur parents
loved their children.

The Stegosaurus Family

150,000,000 B.C.

A proud daddy

TICKET 4,440 POUNDS

The Stegosauruses are my favorite relatives. Aren't they great?
We look a lot alike, don't you think?

Stig blows out two candles

My grandpa told me that the Stegosaurus loved to eat plants.
I wonder if they liked corn as much as I do!

The Triceratops Family

TICKET 27,998 **POUNDS**

Lunchtime

A little gas

The Triceratops family also ate lots of plants.
Pee-ew! They were happy, but gassy!

More gas!

Something is wrong.

But then, millions of years ago, something went terribly wrong.
Some say the weather got too warm for dinosaurs to live.

65,000,000 B.C.

Asteroid

Earthquake

Others say that a burning-hot asteroid crashed onto the earth.
The earth trembled, and everything cracked.
Volcanos fired out lava and ashes in the air.

Volcanic eruption

The end

It turned pitch black. Without sunlight,
plants died. There was hardly any food left.
In the end, all dinosaurs starved to death . . .

Well, almost all dinosaurs.

Because we, the *Gallus gallus domesticuses,* are still running around.

And we're very proud of our dinosaur feet!

You don't still think these are ordinary chicken feet, do you?

SO YOU'RE ACTUALLY A DINOSAUR TOO!
WHAT AN INCREDIBLE STORY.

It might be incredible, but it's really true.
And now you'll have to excuse me . . .

I have an egg to hatch.

Maybe it will be a cute little
Triceratops chicken.

Or a sweet Diplodocus . . .

Wait a second . . .

Could it be . . . ?

Stegosaurus

Diplodocus

Parasaurolophus

Triceratops